Purchase of this book
was made possible by
Douglass Ross
April 2012

We Read
PHONICS™

Robot Man

TREASURE BAY

Parent's Introduction

Welcome to **We Read Phonics**! This series is designed to help you assist your child in reading. Each book includes a story, as well as some simple word games to play with your child. The games focus on the phonics skills and sight words your child will use in reading the story.

Here are some recommendations for using this book with your child:

1 Word Play

There are word games both before and after the story. Make these games fun and playful. If your child becomes bored or frustrated, play a different game or take a break.

Phonics is a method of sounding out words by blending together letter sounds. However, not all words can be "sounded out." **Sight words** are frequently used words that usually cannot be sounded out.

② Read the Story

After some word play, read the story aloud to your child—or read the story together, by reading aloud at the same time or by taking turns. As you and your child read, move your finger under the words.

Next, have your child read the entire story to you while you follow along with your finger under the words. If there is some difficulty with a word, either help your child to sound it out or wait about five seconds and then say the word.

③ Discuss and Read Again

After reading the story, talk about it with your child. Ask questions like, "What happened in the story?" and "What was the best part?" It will be helpful for your child to read this story to you several times. Another great way for your child to practice is by reading the book to a younger sibling, a pet, or even a stuffed animal!

This time, let's read the story together!

LEVEL 4   **Level 4** introduces words with long "e," "o," and "u" (as in *Pete, nose,* and *flute*) and the long "e" sound made with the vowel pairs "ee" and "ea." It also introduces the soft "c" and "g" sounds (as in *nice* and *cage*), and "or" (as in *sports*).

Robot Man

A We Read Phonics™ Book
Level 4

Text Copyright © 2010 by Treasure Bay, Inc.
Illustrations Copyright © 2010 by Jeffrey Ebbeler

Reading Consultants: Bruce Johnson, M.Ed., and Dorothy Taguchi, Ph.D.

We Read Phonics™ is a trademark of Treasure Bay, Inc.

Published by
Treasure Bay, Inc.
P.O. Box 119
Novato, CA 94948 USA

Printed in Singapore

Library of Congress Catalog Card Number: 2010921691

Hardcover ISBN: 978-1-60115-329-6
Paperback ISBN: 978-1-60115-330-2

We Read Phonics™
Patent Pending

Visit us online at:
www.TreasureBayBooks.com

PR 07/10

Robot Man

By Paul Orshoski
Illustrated by Jeffrey Ebbeler

Alphabet Soup

Creating words using certain letters will help your child read this story.

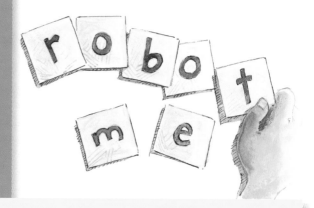

Materials: thick paper or cardboard; scissors; pencils, crayons, or markers; small cooking pot and stirring spoon

1. Cut 40 two x two inch squares from the paper or cardboard and print letter and letter combinations on the squares. Make two each with r, b, t, m, n, ea, ee, w, d, s, c, l, p, u, and c. Make three cards with "a" and "e." Make four cards with "o."

2. Place the letters into a pretend pot of soup and stir the pot! Then, players take turns taking letters from the pot. When a player can make a word by putting his letters together, he makes and reads the word out loud. Once a word is made, the player can use the letters in that word (and other letters) to make new words. If scoring, give a point for each word that is made.

3. Players take turns taking letters and making new words. Once a player has nine letters, he must put one letter back in the pot in order to take another letter.

4. If scoring, the words *robot* and *man* can be bonus words worth an extra point. If a player can make both *robot* and *man* at the same time, he automatically wins!

5. The winner is the first player to score 12 points. Then, put all the letters back into the pretend pot of soup and play again!

Some words that can be made with these letters include *weeds, clean, made, space, speed, cream,* and *sweet.*

Memory

This is a fun way to practice recognizing some sight words used in the story.

1. Write each word listed on the right on two plain 3 x 5 inch cards, so you have two sets of cards. Using one set of cards, ask your child to repeat each word after you. Shuffle both decks of cards together, and place them face down on a flat surface.

2. The first player turns over one card and says the word, then turns over a second card and says the word. If the cards match, the player takes those cards and continues to play. If they don't match, both cards are turned over, and it's the next player's turn.

3. Keep the cards. You can make more cards with other **We Read Phonics** books and combine the cards for even bigger games!

away

you

more

could

some

pull

said

would

down

Pull the weeds and clean the sink.

Toss the trash away. It stinks!

These are jobs my dad must do.

And Mom said I must do them too.

So Dad and I made up a plan...

. . . to make a space-age robot man.

The robot man came in a kit.

Too bad not all the parts would fit.

Dad got the robot man to go.

He made the robot wave hello.

The robot man did all the jobs.

So Dad and I could sit like blobs.

The robot man would hoe and weed.

He drove me home at quite a speed.

He froze us all some ice cream treats.

I have to tell you, life was sweet!

Yes, life was good, and all was swell.
Then robot man went plunk and fell.

The robot man was out of whack.
He put the ice cream down my back.

Those brand new lamps,
I will not miss.

But then from Mom
he stole a kiss.

My mom said there was no excuse.
And robot man had no more use.

So Mom sent us to hit the sack.
And then she sent the robot back.

Word Cross

Creating words from these letters will help your child practice building words like those in this story.

Materials: Use the same letter cards created for Alphabet Soup (see page 2).

1. Place the cards with the letter side down on a table. Each player draws five cards.

2. The first player tries to make a word using the cards. If no word can be made, the player discards one card and draws another card, and it becomes the next player's turn.

3. If the first player can make a word using the cards, the player makes the word going across. After making a word, a player receives one point for each letter used and draws enough cards to maintain five cards.

4. Subsequent words must be built upon words previously made, either across or down, in a crossword pattern. For example, if the first player builds the word *red,* then the next player must build a word going down, using "r," "e," or "d," such as *seed* or *rude.*

5. Consider playing with both players showing their letters and helping each other.

Rhyming

Practicing rhyming words helps children learn how words are similar.

What rhymes with treat?

Sweet!

1. Explain to your child that these words rhyme because they have the same end sounds: *sink, stink, link, mink, pink, rink, think,* and *wink.*

2. Ask your child to say a word that rhymes with *sink.*

3. If your child has trouble, offer some possible answers or repeat step 1. It's okay to accept nonsense words, for example, *bink.*

4. When your child is successful, repeat step 2 with these words:

   plan (possible answers: *can, Dan, fan, man, pan, ran, tan, van*)

   kit (possible answers: *bit, fit, hit, lit, mitt, knit, pit, sit, wit*)

   jobs (possible answers: *blobs, Bobs, globs, lobs, mobs, sobs*)

   weed (possible answers: *bead, seed, deed, feed, heed, lead, need, read*)

   treat (possible answers: *beat, feet, heat, meet, neat, seat, sweet, wheat*)

   whack (possible answers: *back, hack, Jack, knack, pack, rack, sack, tack*)

If you liked **Robot Man,**
here is another **We Read Phonics** book you are sure to enjoy!

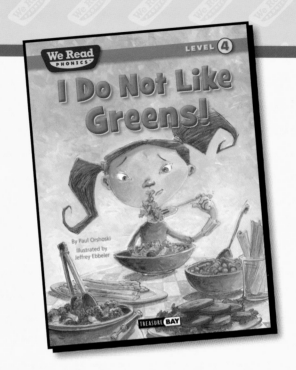

I Do Not Like Greens!

Greens, greens, and more greens! Dad likes to cook, but he will only cook healthy food. What if you want some sweet and fatty junk food? Well, junk food is okay—if you are Dad's dog. But for his little girl, Dad only serves greens and other foods that are good for her. What's a girl to do?

TIME FOR THIS MACHINE TO START KILLING FASCISTS

contentious

Summer 2007

*Cover image and
incidental drawings
by Eleanor Davis*

MOME 8: SUMMER 2007
Published by Fantagraphics Books, 7563 Lake City Way Northeast,
Seattle, Washington, 98115. MOME is copyright © 2007 Fantagraphics
Books. Individual stories are copyright © 2007 the respective artist.
"Young American" © 2007 Émile Bravo, with rights arranged through
Sylvain Coissard Agency. All rights reserved. Permission to repro-
duce material from the book, except for purposes of review and/or
notice, must be obtained by the publisher. Edited by Eric Reynolds
and Gary Groth. Art direction by Adam Grano, covers and MOME
format designed by Jordan Crane. Promoted by Eric Reynolds.

First edition: June 2007.
ISBN: 978-1-56097-847-3. Printed in Singapore.

SUBSCRIBE TO MOME:
Save 10 dollars per year off the cover price.
Rates for a four-issue subscription are as follows:
$49.95 U.S. & Canada only
$54.95 for global surface mail
$69.95 for global air mail

Each issue is carefully boxed prior to being shipped. To subscribe
using your Visa or MasterCard, call us toll-free at 1-800-657-1100 or
visit our website: WWW.FANTAGRAPHICS.COM. Otherwise, send U.S.
check or money order to: MOME SUBSCRIPTIONS, c/o Fantagraphics
Books, 7563 Lake City Way NE, Seattle, WA 98115 USA.

 Visit the new Fantagraphics Bookstore & Gallery in Seattle:
1201 S. Vale St. (at Airport Way).

For a free catalog of comics and cartooning, please telephone
1-800-657-1100 or consult WWW.FANTAGRAPHICS.COM.

EDITORS' NOTES:

a. This eighth volume marks our two-year anniversary. Please send cake to Fantagraphics Books, Seattle, WA.

b. For the second issue in a row, we have two new ongoing contributors to MOME, Ray Fenwick and Joe Kimball, whom we hope will be around for a while. Both are new to the comics scene (this is, astonishingly, Joe's first published work), so be nice to them. And don't miss Ray's website (see his bio in the back of this book); we're appalled that he's escaped our attention this long.

c. Please welcome back Tom Kaczynski, Eleanor Davis, Al Columbia, and Émile Bravo, all making their second contributions to MOME, which pleases us greatly, as does the return of Jonathan Bennett after an issue's absence.

d. This issue concludes Lewis Trondheim's *At Loose Ends*; special thanks to translator Kim Thompson for bringing the work to our attention and facilitating its publication, and to Mr. Trondheim for the privilege of publishing it in MOME.

e. Thanks also to Mr. Thompson for his translation of Émile Bravo's contribution this issue; we wish we could curse in as many languages as he can.

f. Kurt Wolfgang's *Nothing Eve* will return next issue with a meaty chapter, as will Tim Henlsey's *Wally Gropius*. Contrary to what we reported last issue, David Heatley's *Overpeck* is regrettably on what we in the biz call "hiatus" while Mr. Heatley catches up on some other projects, notably a forthcoming collection from St. Martin's Press. We apologize for any inconvenience and will keep you informed.

g. Our next volume will see the debut of a two-part Jim Woodring graphic novella, *The Lute String*, until now previously available only in Japan. This original, 48-page "Frank" story will warp even dedicated Woodring readers, we promise you, and we are honored to publish it.

h. We welcome your letters of comment. Please write us at fbicomix@fantagraphics.com and include "MOME comments" in the subject line.

STICK AND STRING

END

CONTESTANT: (♪Singing ♪ ♪Singing ♪ ♪Singing ♪ ♪Singing)

JUDGE: (INTERRUPTS) OK, ok, all right. I've heard enough.

CONTESTANT: YOU DON'T *UNDERSTAND!* I've fought so _hard_ for this. I... I don't know how to say this, but I KNOW that you know I can _DO THIS._ And I know that you have watched me grow, and I know that you know what it's like to struggle with your weight, to struggle with your music, and I have waited, and I have worked *HARDER,* harder than *ANYBODY,* HARDER THAN *ANYBODY* OUT THERE, and each time I have auditioned you've given me more and more encouragement. I have TAKEN it. I have INTERNALIZED it. I have fought, harder than...than...I ever thought I was even *CAPABLE OF FIGHTING!* And I understand your position, I _do_, but I really in the *depths* of my *soul* believe that you _don't_ _have_ this _RIGHT._ In the _DEPTHS_ of my _SOUL_ I know: IF AMERICA GOT A chance... THAT'S THE ONLY THING YOU HAVEN'T GIVEN ME, is the chance for AMERICA TO VIEW ME, and that's the only thing, because if AMERICA SAW ME, THEY WOULD **LOVE ME**. They would... love me. And before I leave, if there is *anything* I can do to change your mind...

JUDGE: (INTERRUPTS) It didn't work. You were _not_ good enough. Get over it. It's a no. Okay? Bye.

AUDITION ENTRANCE

WAIT... UNTIL CALLED

Lucid Night-mare Part 3

BY SOPH

CRUMB

1.07

We left off with these 3 nobodys awaking from a dream — only they werent sleeping! No, their reality was distorted by a soft, sweet veil of ZION 9...

The word "NIGHT-MARE" would more likely apply to this scene!

You SICK FUCKS!! You LITTLE PIGS! UGN... sniff... You ROB ME, You KIDNAP ME, You FUCKIN DRUG ME and WHERE THE HELL DID YOU TAKE ME?? WHERE AM I?? MAMA...

HEY WAIT WE DIDNT HAVE TO HOOK YOU UP, THAT WAS A GESTURE...

AAH

HEY! DONT FUCKIN SCREAM LIKE THAT... WE'RE ALL GUNNA HAVE A SEIZURE LIKE YOU! JUST CALM DOWN... WE DONT KNOW SHIT, JUST LIKE YOU! WE JUST CAME DOWN LIKE YOU!! IF YOU TAKE THAT SHIT AND WANDER OFF, ANYTHING CAN HAPPEN. THATS WHY I STAY IN BED NORMALLY...

OH NO...DO... DO YOU THINK WE...

WHAT. THINK WE WHAT

I DONT KNOW... I MEAN WE'RE TRAPPED! EITHER BY THE POLICE OR BY OTHER TYPES OF CRIMINALS... BUT... I WONDER IF WE DID SOME THING... UH... MESSED UP OR WHAT?

WHO FUCKING KNOWS

UGH...I HAVE THIS GUILTY FEELING INSIDA ME... UGH!

HEY

SHH... I THINK I HEAR SOMEONE!

WHISPERIN →

HEY SO, WHAT'S ORDERS?... YEH WE GOTS THE WHORE, BUT SHE'S WITH TWO FENUKS..... YEH.... .... YEAH? SURE, SURE... YOU GOT IT. OK.

OH MY FUCKING GOD... OH GOD

SEE, YA CUNT! ITS YOU THEY KNOW, ITS COZ A YOU WERE HERE, YOU —

SHHH

DO YOU BELIEVE DIS SHIT,?!

BULLSHIT JOB! I AINT DOIN' NO MORE FREAKSHOW ACTS! FUCK DAT!

HA HA...FUCKIN WALLOWIN' IN PISS N' SHIT! FACES IN DA BLOOD AND GUTS!

SICK SATAN FREAKS...

DONT REMIND ME!

OH

BLURG...

WHAT??

PISS N' SHIT?!

CLIPCLIPCLIPCLOPCLIPCLOP

WAKE UP MY LITTLE CHICKADEES!! HEH HEH WE'RE LEAVING!!

WHERE?! WHERE ARE WE GOING ??WHO ARE YOU?!

WHAT, YOU DONT REMEMBER?

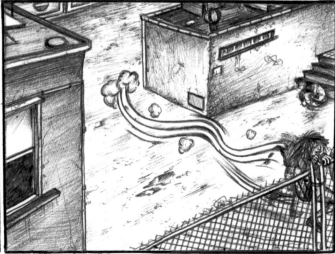

COME ON! OVER HERE

PANT PANT

PANT PANT!! JESUS FUCKING CHRIST!! DONT TELL ME THATS MY GUN??!! DID YOU HAVE IT ON YOU THIS WHOLE TIME??!

YEAH, IT APPEARS SO.... IN MY SOCK!!

HOLY CRAP OF CRAPS, IF THAT GUY'S DEAD, WE'RE ALL FOOD FOR THE PIGS!!

DO YOU THINK HE'S DEAD?

WHO KNOWS?? HEY, JUST GIMME A MINUTE HERE, SANDRA... WHAT COULD YOU HAVE POSSIBLY DONE TO THIS "BOSS" GUY TO HAVE HIM CAPTURE US?!

WHAT DID I DO TO HIM? HA! THAT FUCKER'S A SICK, MURDER-OUS PSYCO AND HE DESERVES TO DIE!! YOU DONT EVEN KNOW—

SO ANYWAYS

ANYWAYS, WHAT? SO I STOLE A TINY BIT OF HIS MONEY, OF HIS FORTUNE! SO—

HOW MUCH?

IT DONT MAKE NO DIFFERENCE.! HE—

HOW MUCH??

EEEH....LITTLE LESS THAN HALF A MIL...PSH.

....

..DAMN....

YEAH WHATEVAH. ..IT TOOK YEARS OF TORTURE...

BUT STILL, THANKS, I MEAN, FOR STOPPIN THAT THUG FROM TAKING ME TO...... .....SHIT! YA HEARD SOMETHIN'??

SHH...SOMEONE'S COMIN'!

LET'S GO!!

SO NOW...DOES THE PATHETIC TRIO GET AWAY? DO THEY EVEN DESERVE TO WIN? THREE USELESS EXCUSES FOR HUMAN BEANS THAT THEY ARE. WELL, YOU MAY OR MAY NOT FIND OUT IN THE NEXT MOME

(IF THE USELESS EXCUSE OF A HUMAN BEAN THAT IS THE AUTHOR DESERVES TO LIVE THUS KEEP DRAWING. SUSPENSE!!

SOPH CRUMB 2/07

a. Ok, she has herpes. It's in legal court documents. Basiaccly, she is a whore.

b. She got a chin implant I think! She had a week chin, so that's good.

c. She only look thinner because of the side shot... plus sucking gut in!!!1!!

d. What is up with teh one eye? Bug-eye, cross-eyed, yuck!

e. No good taste and so ass-ugly it probibley impacts her health.

f. U-G-L-Y looking troll "woman."

TEH THINGS YOU SHOULD KNOW ABOUT THAT BITCH!!!1!1!
BY: THE INTERNET

g. She would be maybe stylish in somewhere as Uzbekistan but not hear O.K.

h. WHOA she has a certain but undeniable inbred quality to her.

i. Dumpy, dumpy, DUMPY.

j. She needs to have her jaw broken and re-set. She looks shih-tzu-ish.

k. Out-dated clothes like a street bum, I hardly can belive it.

m. She is not a true lady I think!!1!! Not CLASSY.

I FELT REBORN... OR RATHER I FELT THE WORLD WAS REBORN AROUND ME...

I WAS WEAK AT FIRST. I COULD ONLY CONSUME LIQUIDS.

I REGAINED STRENGTH RAPIDLY. AND STARTED CRAVING SOLIDS.

THE HOSPITAL PSYCHOLOGIST TOLD ME THAT I HAD "SLEPT" FOR TEN THOUSAND YEARS.

IT WAS SOME KIND OF TRANCE?

YES.

THE FUTURE WAS A LITTLE DISAPPOINTING. I EXPECTED SOMETHING RADICALLY DIFFERENT, NOT A JOB IN AN ADVERTISING AGENCY.

MANY FAMILIAR PRODUCTS WERE STILL AROUND, BUT WITH EXOTIC NEW FLAVORS.

NEW TASTE

AS EXPECTED, TECHNOLOGY PRO-GRESSED. PORTABLE DEVICES WERE MORE POWERFUL AND THINNER THAN EVER BEFORE.

WHO IS THIS?

HOLD

SNAP WRIST

THWIP

READY

THE WORLD WAS FOR SALE AGAIN.

SHOE CITY

SHAPE+ blob

iPILL
INGEST SOUND

NOSTALGIA®

GHOST BEARD

NEW SHAVE

ORO SKY HOMES
AFFORDABLE LUXURY

STRETCH BEAST

ACID WASH
ACID
DETER-GENT

PURE CHOCOLATE LAXATIVE

I GOT AN EXPENSIVE CONDO WITH A BREATHTAKING VIEW, A CUTE GIRLFRIEND (SMART TOO!) ...

... AND A MONOLITHIC TV, WITH MY FAVORITE SHOW: 23RD INTERPLANETARY.

THE DREAMER IS AWAKE!

SUMMON THE LEADER!

NEVER CALL ME LEADER! I AM MERELY THE EMERGENT MANIFESTATION OF THE WILL OF OUR COLLECTIVE DISORDER.

THE ACTION TOOK PLACE ON MARS. THERE WAS SOME KIND OF ZOMBIE REVOLUTION UNDERWAY.

I KNOW. BRING HIM!

THE DREAMER LOOKED LIKE ME, AT LEAST ACCORDING TO MY BRAND NEW GIRLFRIEND.

YOU HAVE DREAMED FOR CENTURIES. YOUR DREAMS ARE THE NEW CURRENCY.

LEADER! WE ARE READY FOR ARMED STRUGGLE!!

SHEATHE YOUR WEAPONS! LISTEN! A SPECTER IS HAUNTING MARS – THE SPECTRE OF CONSUMERISM. THE STORM OF HISTORY IS APPROACHING. ALL THAT IS SOLID MELTS INTO THE AIR.

CONSUMERS OF THE SOLAR SYSTEM, SAVE YOUR RECEIPTS!

THE END OF THE END OF HISTORY HAS ARRIVED. THE TRAUMA OF THE 20TH CENTURY WILL HEAL. THE PYRAMID CITY WILL WITHER AS WE HAVE WITHERED.

THE SHOPPING CENTERS ARE QUIET AND EMPTY, AWAITING OUR RETURN... AND WE WILL RETURN EVERYTHING!

CAR PARKS AWAIT OUR OCCUPATION. WITHOUT AMPLE PARKING SPACE, CHAOS WILL REIGN IN THE STREETS.

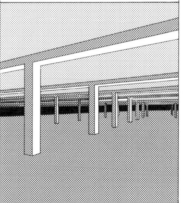

THE OFFICE PYRAMIDS WILL ONCE AGAIN SCREAM WITH THE SILENCE OF TOMBS.

CONSUMER SOCIETY! ACCORDING TO THE LAW OF ETERNAL RETURN, WE DEMAND A REFUND!

WHAT IS THAT INFERNAL NOISE?!

OH...

MY CELLPHONE RANG AND I MULTI-TASKED INTO SOME OTHER REALITY.

SPARE A CREDIT?

IT'S FOR ME...

I DIDN'T KNOW THE NUMBER OF THE CALLER. THE OTHER END OF THE LINE REPLIED WITH RHYTHMIC STATIC LIKE A VACUUM TUBE RADIO TUNED TO THE FREQUENCY OF QUASARS.

HELLO?
HELLO?
HELLO?

I SEE...

YOUR DREAM OF REVOLUTION, LEADING PRESUMABLY, TO SOME UTOPIAN DE- NOUEMENT IS AN INFANTILE CASE OF WISH FULFILLMENT.

UH...

WE ALL DESIRE, BUT CIVILIZATION RE- QUIRES SACRIFICE. IT CONTROLS OUR MOST BRUTAL AGGRESSIVE AND SEX- UAL INSTINCTS. SUBLIME SUBLIMATION.

...ADS DO NOT INTERRUPT AS THEY FILL IN THE BLANKS. THEY FILL THE EMPTINESS OF OUR SOULS. FUN- DAMENTALLY WE ARE EMPTY. NA- TURE ABHORS A VACUUM.

HOW MUCH DO I OWE?

CIVILIZATION SATISFIES DESIRES BY INFLATING THEM. IT'S A TRADE-OFF. SOCIETY CREDITS YOU LIFE AND SECURITY IN EXCHANGE FOR REPRESSION.

CASH? WE PREFER CREDIT MR CAYCE.

I WAS STILL DREAMING. I DECIDED TO RETURN TO THE CONDO.

DEBT, AND WE'RE ALL BORN WITH IT, IS REPAID WITH ALIENATION...

ZIZMOR

PSYCHIC FREUDIAN ASTROLOGY

I LIVED IN THE CONDOMINIUM DISTRICT. THE ULTRA-MODERN HIGH RISES WERE ERECTED IN A SINGLE WEEK OF BUILDING ORGY. INSTANT NEIGHBORHOOD.

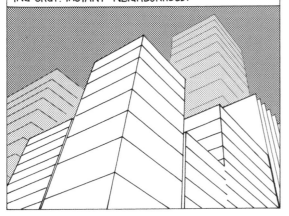

THE STATE OF THE HALLWAYS REFLECTED THE MOOD OF THE RESIDENTS. I WAS MOVING THROUGH THE CORRIDORS OF SOME KIND OF SLOW MOTION APOCALYPSE.

THE APARTMENT LOOKED MORE 21ST CENTURY THAN BEFORE. ETERNAL SAMENESS PERMEATED ALL OBJECTS. THE FUTURE WAS IN RETREAT.

MY GIRLFRIEND WAS DEAD ASLEEP... OR JUST DEAD... SICK... DEFECTIVE? I COULDN'T BE SURE. I WAS NO LONGER SURE WHAT CENTURY THIS WAS.

I DIDN'T KNOW WHAT TO DO SO I JUST SAT DOWN. TIME FLOWED IN NO PARTICULAR DIRECTION.

I'M NOT SURE AT WHICH MOMENT I NOTICED THAT EVERYTHING WAS AN ELABORATE SET CONSTRUCTED OUT OF PAPIER MÂCHÉ. I WAS SURROUNDED BY HOLLOW EFFIGIES.

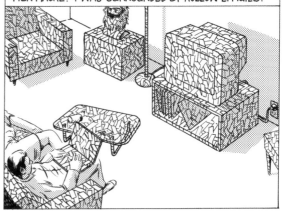

"HI"

I TRIED TO RESIST THE BIOLOGICAL COMPULSION TO EX-CHANGE GENETIC INFORMATION. WE PERFORMED THE TASK MECHANICALLY AND DISPASSIONATELY, LIKE DAMAGED AUTOMATA MIMICKING PORNOGRAPHY.

THE BRIEF MOMENTS POST-ORGASM ARE A STATE OF COMMUNION WITH THE INANIMATE. THE CONSCIOUSNESS WANDERS, ROOTLESS AMONG THE CHEMICAL AND MINERAL COMPONENTS OF THE BODY SEEKING THE MYSTERY OF ITS EXISTENCE.

I TRAVELED IN TIME AGAIN, THIS TIME TO ONE BILLION B.C. IN THE OXYGEN-LESS SKY I SAW A MARTIAN METEOR PENETRATE THE EARTH. THE ORIGIN OF LIFE INFECTED.

SUDDENLY EVOLUTION MAKES SENSE. PROTOPLASMIC CAPITALISM. PROTEIN CURRENCY. AMINO ACID EXCHANGE RATES. MOLECULAR SURPLUS.

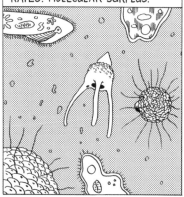

FERAL COMPETITION. CARNIVOROUS CONFLICT. REPTILIAN EXPLOITATION. COLD-BLOODED SHOPPING.

PALEOLITHIC CORPORATIONS. CRO-MAG-NON CAPITAL. NEANDERTHAL PROFITS. VIRILE ENTERPRENEURS.

THROUGH THE AEONS, A THIN THREAD OF MARTIAN DNA HAUNTS THE TERRESTRIAL GENOME.

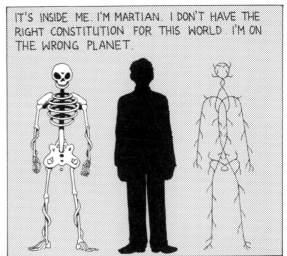

IT'S INSIDE ME. I'M MARTIAN. I DON'T HAVE THE RIGHT CONSTITUTION FOR THIS WORLD. I'M ON THE WRONG PLANET.

WHAT PLANET DO YOU THINK YOU'RE ON MISTER CAYCE?

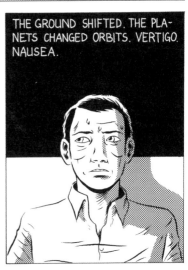

THE GROUND SHIFTED. THE PLANETS CHANGED ORBITS. VERTIGO. NAUSEA.

THE ENTIRE SPACE-TIME CONTINUUM BECAME SUSPECT. THE ZODIAC WAS AN ALIEN BESTIARY. CIVILIZATION WAS AN ANCIENT BURIAL GROUND WITH UNFAMILIAR FUNERARY RITES.

MISTER CAYCE

ASTRAL DISASTER.

WE DON'T HAVE A REFUND POLICY...

SURPLUS GRAVITY, THE COMPOSITION OF THE ATMO-SPHERE, THE ELECTRO-MAGNETIC RADIATION MADE EVERY STEP AN AGONY.

WITH EFFORT I MADE IT UP TO THE APARTMENT.

THE SOUND OF RUNNING WATER SLOWLY DISSOLVED THE MEMORIES OF THE DREAM AND MADAME ŽIŽMOR.

PSSSHH

THE BUOYANCY OF WATER RELIEVED THE PRESSURE OF GRAVITY. THE WORLD DROWNED IN MY TUB.

BUT MARS REMAINS. I CAN FEEL MY HUMANITY MELT AWAY.

THE ALIEN INSIDE ME GROWS STRONGER.

THE FACE ON MARS NODS IN SILENT APPROVAL

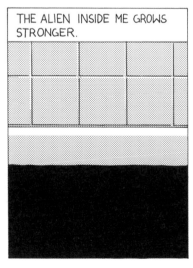

END

1953, somewhere in the Midwest...

Hrunt!

PAF!

HOME RUN!!

WE WIN!

Good one, Billy! Eat your heart out, DiMaggio! That ball's a goner!

HA! HA! Just a lucky break, is all!

YAAY! This'll do wonders for his self-confidence!

Don't tell me he's lacking in that department!

Physically, no, but intellectually he's got a little bit of an inferiority complex.

Oh, really? You mean, scratch the jock and there's nothing underneath?

Bite your tongue, you meanie! Billy is a fine, sensitive young man. All he needs is a special someone by his side to bring it out...

A special someone like you, maybe? Tee-hee! I hope you introduce me to him at the party tomorrow. I'll be the judge of whether he's the man for you!

Grace, you're incorrigible!

HIP! HIP! HOORAY FOR BILLY!

Take care, fellas! I need to get on home, I'll see you tomorrow at Jenny's.

You bet! It's gonna be the blowout of the year!

"Eat your heart out, DiMaggio!" Heh heh!

Howdy, pops! Say hello to the school's star slugger! We just made it to state!

Oh, Billy!

Sometimes I look at you and despair! Is baseball the only thing that matters to you in this world? Are you completely oblivious to the society in which we live?

What?

Here I am, being crushed by this paranoid McCarthyite state which erodes my spirit, and you cheerfully hop into their mold of petit bourgeois America! When are you going to wake up?

Sweetie! He's just a boy!

Great scott! Let him use his brain for once! It's almost as if... AS IF HE ISN'T OUR CHILD!

Calm down! You're exhausted! You don't even know what you're saying!

Okay, fine, Billy, if you're so dead set on bowing down to authority...

Honey!

I forbid you to attend that surprise party tomorrow!

NOOOO!

Next day...

Don't worry, I'm sure your dad'll reconsider.

It ain't fair.

People call him a Communist...

People are blind...

Your dad's much more of a humanist, but in these days of cold war and fear within our oh-so-individualistic society it's the ignorant who rule...

You talk good, Jenny... you ought to go see him.

I was going to suggest it. Just you wait, I'll convince him.

Spiff yourself up, li'l Jenny!

DING! DONG!

Good evening, Mr. Loyd. I'm Jenny Jones, a friend of your son's. May I have a word with you?

Oh, about the party. Come on in.

What a cozy home...

Thanks... I have no idea what you're going to say but my decision is firm...

Mister Loyd, let me be frank. I am not who you believe me to be, a brainless teenager, future housewife, pure product of the American consumer society. I've done some thinking and I fully understand your position.

?

Well... I confess that I'm pleasantly surprised...

2

Please rest assured that I'll do everything in my power to awaken in Billy the love for literature and the arts that burns in me...

I don't know what to say... Billy is a lucky boy... You may succeed where his parents failed...

It's all my fault... I hate myself for never having bonded with him... I am a selfish and cowardly creature. I seek refuge in alcohol...

Don't be so hard on yourself.

I wanted to punish him as I was punished, by squeezing out his lust for life. I hope he'll forgive me... I love him so...

He'll understand, Sir. Thank you for lifting the sanction.

So?

There, it's all fixed.

All you've got to do is play the charm card and you're in like Flynn...

I heard it all. He spilled his guts to you. He's never talked to me like that!

Tsk! Eavesdropping isn't very nice!

You're too closed off, both of you. Learn to share...

Share? What do we have to share?

Everything! For starters, I'm going to take care of your cultural education. I'll loan you some thrilling books.

Books?

Give it a chance, you'll enjoy them! You'll be able to discuss them with your dad, he'll be so pleased! He's an intellectual, you know.

Yeah, I noticed he doesn't like sports.

But that's no good either! Turn him on to the art of baseball!

You think?

Of course I do!

The next day.

What a swell party this is!

I'm glad you like it! Come on, I want to show you something.

Jenny!

I think you chose good!

Never a doubt in my mind!

What was Gracie going on about?

Why, my dress, of course. Step this way...

3

Wow! What a nifty library!

Isn't it, though?

Looks like I've got my work cut out for me! It'll take me a while to plow through all this...

No time like the present to get started! Here you go!

"The Crucible"...

It's about how fear generates paranoia. The writer impugns the very system that oppresses your father.

Arthur Miller... I'll give it a try...

Yes, read, cultivate yourself, because otherwise our society sentences us to live like animals, within the pale monotony of days that all resemble each other.

Then again, between you and me, it's not Arthur Miller who's going out with Marilyn Monroe, but DiMaggio, am I right?

Oh, that's just because she hasn't met him yet...

It's true! He's even cuter holding a book! Billy, come and dance the bebop with me! Giggle!

Say no! That floozy is capable of anything!

HA! HA! Sorry, I don't know that dance!

Midnight. After a memorable evening, Billy has to go home to bed.

CLONG!

Thanks, guys! I see lights on in my house. My dad's still up, I guess. I'll go show him my new book!

DAD!!

What were you gonna do with that gun?

I'm a monster! Let me end it!

But dad, I love you!

Sob! Forgive me for all my mistakes, son! I love you too!

I'm gonna get educated, dad! Jenny's opened my eyes...

She's a swell girl!

Yes! And you'll come watch me play baseball and you'll be proud of me, otherwise it'll be PANDEMONIUM! Will you come, dad? Will you?

I promise! Everything will be different now!

But Dad did not keep his promise... nor did Billy, in fact, ever crack open that book...

CHTAK!

Fuck!

SHIT YEAH!!

Fucker!

Here, lemme jam my thumb up your ass, DiMaggio! You deserve a treat for that swing! Better'n pussy, ain't it!

HA! HA! Leggo, you faggots!

Bravo, Billy! You kick ass!

If he wields his cock like he wields that bat...

Shit, no! He's too much of a pansy! But they do kinda look alike... His is this big!

Oh man! Get out of here! You're shitting me!

Well, listen, I'll let you be the judge tomorrow at this little shindig I'm throwin'...

That's right! Can I borrow him then? Super! My mouth is already watering!

Jesus, you really are the queen of sluts!

We fucked 'em good! Fucked 'em good! Fucked 'em, fucked 'em good! ♫

Awrite, you guys just keep right on takin' it up the ass in the locker room! I'll see you again at the party at Jenny's.

Hey Billy! How 'bout a li'l fisting for the road?

Fucked 'em good! Fucked 'em, fucked 'em, fucked 'em good! ♫

Hey, jackoff!

Oh, shit!

One a' these days I'm gonna kick your scrawny little cherry ass!

Cherry?

Yeah, cherry! And you sure ain't gonna pop that baby tomorrow unless your baseball buddies plug your hole 'cause I've got a little surprise for you!

Shut your hole, you wino!

Who the fuck asked you? See my hand? You want a taste, you dumb cunt?

No! Stop! Not in the face!

I'm gonna deal with your mother! Meanwhile, your party, it's a fuckin' non-starter, OK?

Ulp!

You can't go. So take your ass straight to bed!

DICKHEAD!

Next day...

Goddamn! That old fossil of yours is a regional champ at fucking up our evenings.

Cock-sucker!

Sometimes I feel like grabbing his gun and offing him...

Oh please, spare me...

Anyway, we're in the shit. Gotta find some way of talking him out of it. Okay, this time, I think there's only one...

One way out? I really don't see how...

Of course you don't. Leave it to me, Billy. I got it covered.

If this doesn't give him a boner...

HONK

Evening, Mister Loyd. I think the last time I came by I forgot my handkerchief.

Your handkerchief? C'mon in, kiddo...

Your wife is out?

Uh... No, she's in the hospital. Fell against the closet door. Why?

Oh! No reason! Actually, it's not my handkerchief I lost, it's my panties! We've got to find 'em 'cause my pussy's freezing and I prefer my pussy hot. Could you maybe help me out with that, Mr. Loyd?

?

Fuckin' a! I b'lieve the two of us're gonna have us a ball.

6

The End

MEDITATION
on the GRID
·

Jonathan Bennett

MOME
FANTAGRAPHICS BOOKS
Seattle

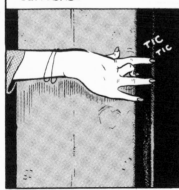

TIC

PICK PICK

I DON'T HAVE THE NAILS YOU NEED TO PEEL THIS STUFF OFF.

. . .

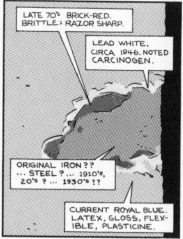

LATE 70's BRICK-RED. BRITTLE; RAZOR SHARP.

LEAD WHITE, CIRCA 1946. NOTED CARCINOGEN.

ORIGINAL IRON??
... STEEL?... 1910's,
20's?... 1930's??

CURRENT ROYAL BLUE. LATEX, GLOSS, FLEX-IBLE, PLASTICINE.

hmm?

THAT GUY IS **BLASTING** HIS HEADPHONES!

WHAT'S THAT HE'S LISTEN-ING TO?

OH! I **KNOW** THAT SONG.

THAT HERRING-BONE TWEED ONLY **COM-POUNDS** MY FRUSTRATION.

hmm hmm hmm...

THE TEXTILE EQUIVELENT OF BAD TELEVISION RECEPTION.

OH, THE **TRAIN** IS COMING! THAT OUGHT TO HELP ME HONE IN ON THE MYSTERY MELODY **TRUMPETING** IN THAT GUY'S EARS.

MMM.... IT FEELS **OKAY** PRESSED INTO THIS BEAM!

RUMBL E RUM

LIKE WHEN I WAS LITTLE AND I WOULD **SQUEEZE** MYSELF INTO THE GAP BETWEEN MY MATTRESS AND THE WALL.

AT SUCH CLOSE RANGE MY WALL-PAPER, A GRID MADE OF LINES OF DIFFERENT COLORS, WOULD BECOME THREE-DIMENSIONAL.

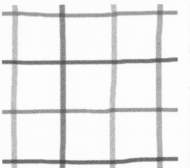

BEFORE MY CROSS-EYES THEY HOVERED LIKE WIRES, JUST INCHES APART FROM EACH OTH-ER, WEAVING A FENCE THAT SEPARATED ME FROM AN IN-FINITE BEIGE FIELD.

I'D JUST LAY THERE IN THE GUTTER, FOR **GOD KNOWS** HOW LONG, MED-ITATING ON THE GRID.

RUMBLE RUMBLE

STEP

THAT GRID'S **STILL GOT IT.**

MAYBE **THAT'S** WHAT I NEED...

SOME NEW TARGET TO FOCUS MY ATTENTION ON AS I TUNE OUT.

A NEW GRID I CAN **DRIFT** INTO...

LATER, I COULD TRY TO **RE-CREATE** THAT OLD PAPER PATTERN AT HOME ON MY COMPUTER.

OR, I CAN **RAZOR** A SQUARE OFF THE WALL OF MY OLD ROOM IN MY PARENTS' HOUSE.

UNLESS IT'S AS SIMPLE AS GETTING A DECENT PHOTOGRAPH...

SLAM

OKAY OKAY! I'M SORRY TO **DISTURB** ALL Y'ALL... MY **YOUNG ASSOCIATE** AND I HAVE GOT TO **DANCE!!**

WE **WILL** NEED YOUR COOPERATION IN **CLEARING** THE **DANCE FLOOR!**

BOOM TST BOOM TST BOMP BOMP BOMP THUMP

HEY. I'VE SEEN THIS PAIR BEFORE. THEY DO THAT OLD DANCING MIDGET THING. HUH.

pft!

OH, THAT'S **GREAT.** I **NEVER** GET TIRED OF THAT ACT.

WISH I HAD MY CAMERA ON ME.

AND THEN

A FLIP...

OVER...

"HERRINGBONE" DOESN'T TAKE IT WELL, AND A MUMBLED, DISINGENUOUS APOLOGY FROM THE BOYS DOESN'T HELP.

UP! LOOKS LIKE IT'S TIME FOR THE BIG FINALE ...

AND **UP!** BUT SOMETHING'S NOT RIGHT ...

#@!%

?!

I'M CURIOUS ABOUT HOW THIS WILL ALL PLAY OUT, BUT THE TRAIN HAS LURCHED TO A STOP AND THIS IS WHERE I GET OFF.

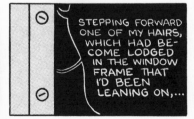

STEPPING FORWARD ONE OF MY HAIRS, WHICH HAD BE-COME LODGED IN THE WINDOW FRAME THAT I'D BEEN LEANING ON,...

THE LITTLE GUY, WHO LOOKED LIKE *THE YELLOW KID* IN THAT GIANT T-SHIRT, BACKED UP TO WHERE I WAS STANDING AND PAUSED FOR A MOMENT, BOUNCING ON HIS HEELS...

...

OOF

!

OH OH OH OH OH

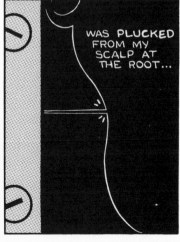

WAS **PLUCKED** FROM MY SCALP AT THE ROOT...

HIDE & WATCH ME

PART ONE: *In the cabin ~*

WHERE IN WANTS & NEEDS BECOME...YES!

1-2. "CLEAN MY CAGE OR I'LL TELL YA' THINGS
YA' AINT NEVER WANNA HEAR"
2a. I'MA TELL YA' 'BOUT ' YER MAW'...
2b. YER GRANDMAW
2c. AND YA' GREAT GRANDMERMAW
2a. YER PA
2b. YER GRANDPA (GERPAW)
2c. YER GREAT GRAN... ~KICK~
3. "SHUT UP! SHUT UP OR I'LL CHOP YOU
INTO PIECES." (HOW SHE FOUND US)
4. OUR WORLD SET INTO MOTION (IT LOOKS
LIKE FALLING SNOW)
5. "OOH IT FELT LIKE WE FELL FO' TWO-
HUNNED YERS ♪♪♪
6. THE LAND COULD FINALLY BE WORKED...
7. INTO A TIGHTLY-KNIT COMMUNITY.
8. A NEW COLLECTOR. OUR NEW HOME.
(HIS FATHER. HIS MOTHER.)
9. "...THE FIRST ONE THAT MOVES."
~FREE AT LAST. LET'S HIDE AND WATCH.
10. A MAN EMPTIES HIS CARS ASHTRAY
INTO THE STREET AT A TRAFFIC LIGHT.
11. THE RETALIATION WAS SEVERE.

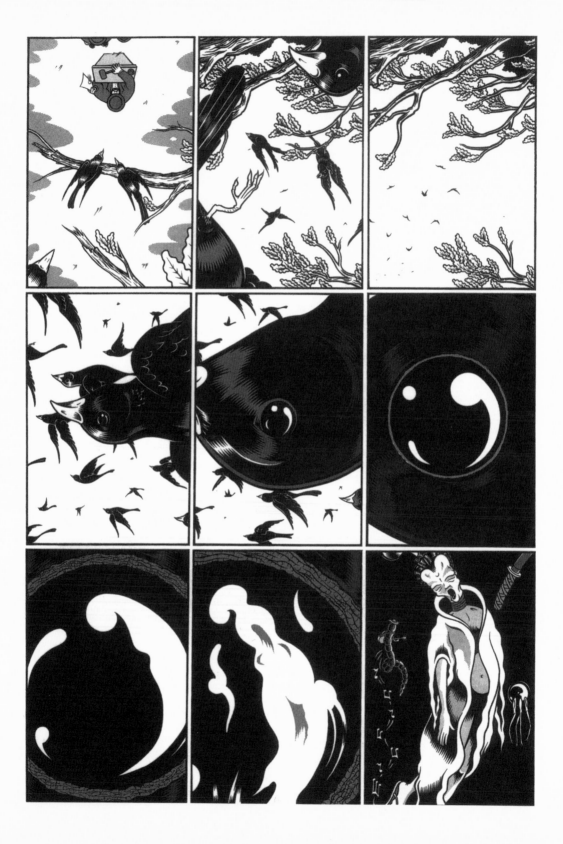

AT LOOSE ENDS, PART THREE

by Lewis Trondheim

TUESDAY, AUGUST 3RD. 9:00 A.M. LOCAL TIME: LUZ, PORTUGAL.

AFTER A THREE-WEEK PERIOD DURING WHICH i BEGAN WORK ON TWO ALBUMS AND APPLIED FOR A JOB AS THE EDITOR OF A COMICS LINE, NOW i'M GEARING UP FOR A THREE-WEEK VACATION...

... WITH THE SFAR FAMILY.

i saw Spiegelman and posed him your question about how cartoonists age.

He said you only quit drawing for a very brief time but he quit for 10 years...

HE QUOTED CRUMB: "COMICS ARE A YOUNG MAN'S GAME. BECAUSE CARTOONISTS BURN OUT QUICKLY. ONCE THEY'VE TURNED 30 THEY DO THE SAME THING OVER AND OVER AGAIN."

BUT SPIEGELMAN WENT ON TO SAY THIS IS HARDLY EXCLUSIVE TO COMICS. HEMINGWAY COMMITTED SUICIDE BECAUSE HE WAS WORRIED ABOUT REPEATING HIMSELF.

HE SAYS WHAT KEEPS CALCIFICATION AT BAY FOR HIM IS THAT HE DOESN'T REMEMBER HIS EARLIER BOOKS ANY MORE.

WITH EVERY NEW BOOK, HE HAS TO LEARN HOW TO DRAW ALL OVER AGAIN SPECIFICALLY FOR THAT BOOK.

HE SAYS THE DIFFERENCE BETWEEN US IS THAT WE WRITE LIKE WE DRAW.

HE NEVER DRAWS ASIDE FROM WHEN HE'S DOING HIS COMICS. WE DON'T EVEN THINK ABOUT OUR DRAWING.

Oh, i also ran into Wolinsky. He's getting ready to do his first real comic strip, complete with ruled panel borders, the whole nine yards.

HE GREETED ME AT "CHARLIE HEBDO" BY TELLING ME IT WOULD DO ME GOOD TO CREATE SOME EDITORIAL CARTOONS, LIKE A VACATION FROM COMICS.

HE ALSO SAID THAT IN COMICS YOU ALWAYS END UP MAKING PRETTY DRAWINGS TO PLEASE THE READER OR THE PUBLISHER.

AFTER A WHILE IT CEASES TO BE GENUINE BECAUSE YOU START ADDING ALL THESE FRILLS, IT BECOMES A MATTER OF CRAFT AND THAT'S WHAT CALCIFIES IT.

WHEN YOU'RE DOING EDITORIAL CARTOONS YOU'RE NOT TRYING TO MAKE A PRETTY DRAWING, YOU'RE AIMING TO PUT ACROSS A POINT.

BUT YOU DO MAKE MORE MONEY DOING COMICS.

THURSDAY, AUGUST 5TH. 5:00 P.M. --
THE LAGOS ZOO.

A short break.

Drawing from nature seems to be an inexhaustible resource.

No script.

Not a thought for your ego.

Screwing up your drawing is a risk you take.

"When me no happy me always do this."*

if you're afraid of losing, stay out of the game.

MAYBE i OUGHT TO DRAW A DISTINCTION AMONG WRITERS, ARTISTS, AND FULL-ON CARTOONISTS. THEY CAN'T ALL AGE IN THE SAME WAY ...

ALTHOUGH...

IN FACT, CARTOONISTS DON'T REALLY AGE IN THE SAME WAY.

* SEE THE TINTIN ALBUM "PRISONERS OF THE SUN."

ALONG THE LINES OF FORTUNE 500 COMPANIES: THE BIGGER THEY GET, THE LESS CURIOUS AND RECEPTIVE THEY BECOME. WHILE THE WORLD EVOLVES THEY JUST QUIT EVOLVING WITH IT.

THEY ASSUME THEIR PROFITABILITY IS IMMUTABLE. THEY'RE STODGY AND UTTERLY ARROGANT.

AND THEY GO UNDER ...

NO MATTER THEIR SIZE.

SAME THING FOR THE GREAT EMPIRES. MESOPOTAMIAN, ROMAN, OTTOMAN ...

AND THE GREAT EUROPEAN KINGDOMS HAD TO ADAPT OR DIE.

EVERYTHING CREATED BY HUMANS IS INHERENTLY HUMAN.

THE UNITED STATES AND LIBERAL CAPITALISM FACE THE SAME FATE.

THERFORE, ADAPTATION IS KEY FOR THE SURVIVAL OF OUR SPECIES.

THIS PAST MONDAY, PTILUC CAME BY TO SEE ME.

HE SEEMS PRETTY CAUGHT UP IN THE BOOK'S POINTS.

i set up a meeting for you with Tibet and Gotlib at Tibet's, the evening before the Solliés-ville festival.

Awesome... want to read what i've come up with so far?

The main reason Hemingway killed himself was because he felt his ability to write books as good as his earlier ones was eroding.

Jack London, same thing... he pushed the link between his life and his life's work even further by killing himself just like his hero Martin Eden did, all because he didn't want to decline...

He got himself a little boat, sailed out to sea and went down with it.

Speaking for myself, the album i'm finishing up now, i can tell that i'm having a harder time with it.

in the old days, the ending would come to me pretty easily in this sort of magical and thrilling moment.

Now it's more of a slog.

Fortunately, i co-wrote a whole bunch of episodes for a TV project that never got off the ground over ten years ago, and now i dig into it, i rediscover, i rework, i've got enough for at least another 20 years thanks to these provisions.

I DID DERIVE ENORMOUS PLEASURE FROM THE SHEER ACT OF DRAWING BETWEEN 1962 AND 1971.

THEN, WITH "L'ÉCHO DES SAVANES," OUR FREEDOM INCREASED SO MUCH COMPARED TO "PILOTE," AND THAT WAS A BLAST.

MY TROUBLES BEGAN WITH "FLUIDE GLACIAL." I WAS WEARING TWO HATS, CARTOONIST AND PUBLISHER. IT WAS REALLY HARD TO RUN THE MAGAZINE AND THEN GO HOME AND DRAW COMICS.

AND WHEN YOU HAVE A MAG OF YOUR OWN YOU'VE GOT RESPONSIBILITIES ... YOU CAN'T JUST FOLLOW YOUR WHIMS.

IN "FLUIDE" #1, I DID A STORY WHERE I APPLIED EVERYTHING I'D LEARNED UP TO THAT POINT.

IN FACT, THE ONLY STORY FROM THE "FLUIDE" PERIOD I'M PLEASED WITH IS THE ONE WITH THE LITTLE PRINCE.

AND IN #2 OR #3, I DID A STORY ABOUT DURANDAL THAT I DICKED AROUND WITH TOO MUCH. I COMPENSATED FOR SOME SHORTCOMING WITH AN ACCUMULATION OF DETAILS AND JOKES.

I ENDED UP DOING GAI-LURON IN HIS UNDERWEAR. ON THE LAST PAGE OF THE ALBUM THE COUPLE WANDERS OFF AND MY GOTLIB CHARACTER STAYS BEHIND ...

ODDLY ENOUGH, THAT HAPPENED RIGHT AS MY DAUGHTER WAS TURNING EIGHTEEN ...

i HAD OTHER QUESTIONS i WANTED TO ASK AND OTHER POINTS TO DELVE DEEPER INTO, LIKE THIS iDEA DELPORTE BROUGHT UP ABOUT THE NEED FOR SOME AUTHORITY AGAINST WHICH TO REBEL ...

BUT SENSING A CERTAIN SKITTISHNESS IN GOTLiB, i STOPPED THERE.

MAYBE i WAS WRONG IN iMAGINING A QUAVER IN HiS VOICE, OR AN INCREASING NERVOUSNESS ... MAYBE i WAS PROJECTING TOO MUCH OF MY OWN AGEING SELF ONTO MY INTERLOCUTOR ...

and ... uh ... not drawing any more ...

uh

THURSDAY SEPTEMBER 2ND.

TiBET iS THE COMPLETE OPPOSITE OF GOTLiB. HE'S 73 (ABOUT FOUR YEARS OLDER THAN GOTLiB), HE'S PUBLISHED 67 RiC HOCHET ALBUMS AND 68 CHICK BiLL ALBUMS, AND HE'S WORKING AWAY ON THE NEXT VOLUME OF EACH ...

it's my escape. i gotta work.

And i have responsibilities toward my collaborators.

PLUS, HAVING A BACKGROUND ARTIST KEEPS ME FRESH, i DON'T HAVE TO DRAW ANYTHING COMPLICATED ANY MORE ...

SO iT STILL GiVES ME ENDLESS PLEASURE.

i ALWAYS DREAMED OF DiRECTING MOVIES OR BEING ON STAGE, WHICH MUST BE WHY MY FAVORITE PART iS MAKING MY CHARACTERS ACT ... i REALLY GET A KICK OUT OF THAT.

FRANQUIN ONCE SAID, "THE MOST FUN I EVER HAD WAS AS AN ACTOR UP ON STAGE, AT SCHOOL."

HE WAS NOT CHEERFUL BY NATURE, BUT HE WAS PEERLESS AT MAKING HIS CHARACTERS ACT.

FRANQUIN WAS DOING DE FUNÈS WHILE HERGÉ WAS DOING ALEC GUINNESS.

IT BECOMES OBVIOUS TO ME THAT TIBET HAS NEVER REALLY GIVEN ANY THOUGHT TO THE ISSUE OF CARTOONISTS' AGEING. MAYBE IT'S A CERTAIN NAIVETE THAT KEEPS HIM FRESH ...

FACT IS, ONE CAN'T SPEAK OF ANY ARTISTIC DECLINE BETWEEN THE FIRST AND THE SIXTY-SEVENTH VOLUME OF "RIC HOCHET." REGARDLESS OF WHAT ONE'S OPINION OF IT IS, IT STAYS AT PRETTY MUCH THE SAME LEVEL ...

TIBET CONFIRMS THAT LE LOMBARD WAS POPULATED BY PARTY ANIMALS AND HORNDOGS, AND DUPUIS BY DEPRESSED ALCOHOLICS.

AT DUPUIS, THE WIVES ACCOMPANIED THE CARTOONISTS TO CONVENTIONS AND TO THE ANNUAL COMPANY DINNER. AT LE LOMBARD, DINNERS WERE STAG, AND EVERYONE ENDED UP AT THE BAR IN THE WEE HOURS.

ONE MIGHT TALK OF CORPORATE CULTURES ...

- EVEN HERGÉ AND JACOBS WERE FLIRTS...
- GREG WAS A PICK-UP ARTIST, BUT NOT A VERY SUCCESSFUL ONE, HE CAME ACROSS AS A LETCH.
- THERE WAS A CARTOONIST WHO ARRIVED IN ANGOULEME, HE RAN INTO A GIRL AT THE TRAIN STATION AND THAT WAS THE LAST WE SAW OF HIM.
- MITTEI, WHO'S NOT MUCH TO LOOK AT, MOVED TO DUPUIS AND NOW HE'S DRINKING ...

it might also be a matter of creative capital.

Right, right... you have to know how to avoid spending all of it.

And there's complementary risks, as well. Either you pace yourself, you hold back, but you risk getting bogged down.

Or you go for broke all at once to get ahead and maybe you find yourself high and dry.

European cartoonists "qui est qui"

ALEXIS

Late 1960s-1970s artist who worked mainly for *Pilote*. Collaborated with Gotlib on a number of projects, including the super-hero parody "Superdupont" up until his death in 1977. (Never published in English except for a handful of pages in the first three issues of *Heavy Metal*.)

ENKI BILAL

Known for his lush, highly-detailed science fiction work, this Yugoslavian expat illustrated a series of SF stories written by Valerian scribe Pierre Christin for *Pilote*, beginning in the mid-1970s. Many of these subsequently appeared in *Heavy Metal* magazine in English and have been released (and re-released) as albums, including *The Black Order Brigade*, *The Town That Didn't Exist*, and *The Nikopol Trilogy*. Boasts a second career as a feature film director, starting with *Bunker Palace Hotel* (1989) and *Tykho Moon* (1997). Currently working on the (possibly four-volume) "Beast Trilogy" of albums.

FRED BLANCHARD

Co-creator (with Olivier Vatine) of the science fiction series "Aquablue" and the "Série B" line for Editions Delcourt. (Never published in English.)

CHARLES BERBERIAN

Half of the Dupuy/Berberian duo, co-creators of "Mr. Jean." (See MOME #7.)

JEAN-CLAUDE DENIS

French cartoonist. Started out in *Pilote* in 1977, has published a number of albums from a variety of publishers. (Never published in English.)

ANDRÉ FRANQUIN

Spirou, Gaston Lagaffe, *Idées Noires*. (See MOME #6.)

GOTLIB

Gotlib discusses his career in this installment. (Also see MOME #7.)

MICHEL (MIKE) GREG

If Stan Lee was French and could draw he'd be the late Greg, the superhumanly prolific and versatile (and skillful) editor, writer and cartoonist whose 52-year career defies summary. As far as English language readers are concerned, one of his "Achille Talon" albums (*Walter Melon: Magnesia's Treasure*) was released in 1981 by Dargaud USA, and one of the *Spirou* stories he wrote, *Z Is For Zorglub*, was released in 1995 by Fantasy Flight — both out of print.

HERGÉ

Tintin, of course (see MOME #6).

EDGAR PIERRE JACOBS

Creator of the series "Blake et Mortimer" (see MOME #7).

MATHIEU LAUFFRAY

Young French cartoonist best known for *Prophet*, done for the Humanoïdes Assoiiés. Worked on the blockbuster conspiracy-kung-fu-werewolf epic *Le Pacte des loups* (*Brotherhood of the Wolf*), directed by his friend Christophe Gans. American readers may have glimpsed Lauffray's comics work on covers for Dark Horse *Star Wars* comics.

PATRICE LECONTE

Best known as a director of fine arthouse French movies (*Monsieur Hire*, *Intimate Strangers*, *The Widow of Saint-Pierre*), Leconte started out as a cartoonist for magazines like *Pilote* and *Fluide Glacial* in the 1970s. His film collaboration with Gotlib was the 1976 *Les Vécés étaient fermés de l'intérieur* ("*The Toilets Were Locked from Inside*"), which is not available in the U.S. (His comics work has never published in English, and is in fact not available in French either.)

FRANK MARGERIN

French cartoonist, creator of the rock-'n'-rolling Lucien. Received the Angouleme Grand Prix in 1992. (Never published in English, except for a few stories in *Heavy Metal* in the late 1970s.)

MITTEÏ

Journeyman Belgian cartoonist, often as an assistant or writer, active from 1955 to his death in 2001. Once worked as the accompanist for Jacques Brel. (Never published in English.)

PTILUC

"Pacush Blues." (See MOME #7.)

THIERRY ROBIN

French cartoonist whose series include *Koblenz* and *Rouge de Chine*. Collaborated with Lewis Trondheim on *Le Petit Père Noël*, released in English by NBM under the title *Li'l Santa* (as well as its follow-up, *Happy Halloween, Li'l Santa*).

JEAN-MARC ROCHETTE

French cartoonist, broke into comics in 1976, best known for drawing the epic graphic novel *Le Transperceneige* after the original artist Alexis died. Also created Edmond le Cochon. Most recent work is the U.S./U.K.-based trilogy *Triomphe à Hollywood*/*Scandale à New York*/*Panique à Londres*, co-created with writer Pétillon. (Never published in English.)

JOANN SFAR

Dungeon, *Little Vampire*, *Vampire Loves*, and *The Rabbi's Cat*. (See MOME #6.)

JEAN TABARY

Best known as the creator of the 1001-Nights comedy series "Iznogoud" (written by René Goscinny until his death in 1977, thereafter by Tabary). (Never published in English.)

TIBET

Co-creator of "Ric Hochet" and "Chick Bill." (See MOME #7.)

ALBERT UDERZO

Co-creator of *Asterix* (with writer René Goscinny), as well as other series including the pilot drama "Tanguy et Laverdure" and the *Asterix*-ish 18th century French-colonizers-and-American Indians series "Oumpah-Pah;" neither is available in English (but the entirety of *Asterix* is).

YOANN

Young French cartoonist, creator of Toto the Platypus. Also drew a "Donjon Monstres" volume for Trondheim and Sfar. U.K. readers may have seen his "Phil Kaos" and "Dark Boris" series in *Deadline* and *Inkling*.

For samples of work and more extensive biographies of these cartoonists, check out www.lambiek.net, from which much of the information on these pages has been shamelessly pilfered.

LUST AIN'T JUST SO STOP OVER-ESTIMATIN YOURSELF!

i love my baby sitter

SOPH CRUMB. FEB 21 '07.

AN INTERVIEW WITH
ELEANOR DAVIS

ABOVE, FROM SKETCHBOOK.

Eleanor Davis, whose parents she describes affectionately as "kind of hippies," was born in 1983 and grew up in Tucson, Arizona, where she spent 12 years attending a "hippie school…where you're allowed to do pretty much whatever you want." As it happens, she wanted to be a cartoonist, an ambition cultivated by her parents who "were super-duper into art stuff in general," and specifically comics; her mother introduced her to John Stanley's *Little Lulu* (in the big Another Rainbow hardcover series) and her father, who was more obsessive about his love of comics, introduced her to many more. She grew up in a household full of comics and artists such as old *MAD*s, *Pogo*, *Krazy Kat*, *Little Nemo*, *Popeye*, *Tintin*, *The Kin-der-Kids*, Larry Gonick, Raymond Briggs, *The Spirit* and, later, Peter Bagge and the Hernandez Brothers. Whew.

She started doing her own mini-comics when she was 15 or 16 after her close high school friend Kate Guillen introduced her to John Porcellino's work. After she'd graduated high school, her parents did not give her the patented parental lecture about the need for career, success, and money-making and instead told her: "Do whatever you want!" Which she proceeded to do. She attended The Savannah College of Art & Design from 2001 to 2006, and our story picks up at that point.

My introduction to her work was her self-published comic, *The Beast Mother*, a short story that exhibited what I learned would be an Eleanor Davis trademark: pitch-perfect visual rhythms and storytelling continuity in the service of a story of a story that resonated with hidden meanings. She has appeared in two issues of *MOME* to date, and may she continue to do so through the run of the book.

— *Gary Groth, March, 2007*

GARY GROTH: *Why did you choose to go to SCAD [Savannah College of Art & Design] over other schools?*

ELEANOR DAVIS: I got out of high school and I just didn't want to do any real schoolwork ever again. I suppose a lot of people feel like that. And because my parents were super-nice... Well, they spoil me. [*Laughs*] They didn't say, "You gotta go to a real school," they said "Do whatever you want!" There was only, at the time, SVA [School of Visual Arts] and SCAD offering a comics program [that I was aware of], which is what I really wanted to do, and I think that SVA made you take ceramics, and I thought "Fuck that." [*Laughter*] What's ceramics got to do with comics? [*Laughs*] So, I went to SCAD.

GG: *[Laughs] Ceramics was part of the mandatory curriculum at SVA?*

ED: I think so.

GG: *How odd.*

ED: That's in my vague memories. My angry 18-year-old memories.

GG: *So, tell me what that experience was like, tell me what the curriculum was like and any stand-out teachers you had.*

ED: It's kind of hard to describe... By far the greatest thing about going to SCAD was that a lot of my fellow students were just spectacular. I got the opportunity to meet all these artists my own age that are just fantastic. Some of them are geniuses, really. That was invaluable, to be around people like that. And just being able to focus on comics for so long was really great. I mean, if I hadn't gone to school for comics I wouldn't be a cartoonist right now. Because I wasn't a very good artist. I've never been an innately talented artist. I was always all right, you know, but I was never particularly good. I wasn't one of those kids who could just draw. I still can't. I still struggle a lot with drawing.

GG: *Did you have art classes in high school?*

ED: Well, it was a hippie school. So, we had an art center where you went to do art, but it wasn't super-structured. I was able to do all the art that I wanted but it wasn't 'til SCAD... the thing is, I'm really competitive, you know? So I showed up at SCAD saying "All I'll ever need is my ballpoint. I can make great works of literature, like John Porcellino, with my ballpoint pen. Craft is the enemy." Which, of course, would have been terrible. I would have been doing third-rate John Porcellino knockoffs for the rest of my life. Going to SCAD I was forced to compete with all these kids whose biggest dream was to be Rob Liefeld, you know?

[*Laughs*] And I couldn't just back down... I had to try and beat them at their own game. So I learned a lot about traditional inking and traditional drawing. I never would have learned perspective, composition, anatomy, all that stuff, otherwise. And now I know how to do all that, it's just invaluable for storytelling. So I'm really thankful that I was kind of pushed into this situation where I was forced to study all the tools of cartooning... I would have written a lot of them off otherwise.

GG: *So, the school taught you an enormous amount about craft.*

ED: Mmm-hmm. Yeah. I mean it was mostly kids who were interested in manga and superheroes, but then there was this handful of these real close friends I had that were doing just amazing work.

GG: *Anybody we would know now?*

ED: Well, there's Drew [Weing]...

GG: *He's a good friend, right?*

ED: He's my boyfriend.

GG: *Yeah, I know.* [Laughs]

ED: Yeah. He had graduated before I showed up, but ... I showed up, and at first I didn't know any

other cartoonists, and I'm kind of brassy...

GG: *Are you?*

ED: He had these mini-comics at the local comic book shop, and I wanted a boyfriend. I read some of his mini-comics and I thought "I'm gonna make this guy be my boyfriend." [*Laughs*] I found somebody who knew him, and made him introduce us, and we've been dating for four years.

GG: *That's pretty great.*

ED: Yeah, I'm bossy like that.

GG: *So you knew you wanted him to be your boyfriend based on his work.*

ED: Yep. There've been a lot of cartoonists who I've wanted to be my boyfriend based on their work, but Drew's the only one I actually wound up meeting and dating.

GG: *I guess you don't want to give me a list of the other guys...*

ED: No, I think that would make them... It would be awkward at conventions. [*Pause.*] They'd avoid me. In fear.

GG: *Or the opposite.* [Davis laughs] *How was SCAD structured in terms of its curriculum? Is it all about cartooning, or does it branch out into other modes of art; painting...?*

ED: Well, the thing that's problem-

atic about SCAD is that it's really huge. It's a giant art school. And it has tons and tons and tons of different majors, you know? The sequential art program is just this real small program within it. Well, it's actually relatively big, but it's comparatively inconsequential, and it's thought to be dorky. I might have told people I was an illustration major a couple times, because I didn't want to say I was a sequential art major.

GG: *Sequential art major. How many students would be in that department?*

ED: I don't know. It's been growing a huge amount, I think that, at least... [*Calls to Drew*] Hey, Drew, do you know how many kids are in the sequential art department nowadays? Like six hundred? At least six hundred, maybe more. I'd have to look it up.

GG: *Holy shit, that's a lot.*

ED: It is a lot. It's growing really fast... It wasn't that big when I started. A lot of it is because of manga.

GG: *That's potentially 590 really bad cartoonists.*

ED: Yeah, but some of them are really good. And they're all really well-meaning. They're all nice kids. I think a lot of it is because of the manga thing. When I started I would be the only girl in any class. Or one of two girls. And by

the end, after four or five years, it was totally split down the middle between guys and girls. And all the girls were into manga, of course.

GG: *And you would attribute their interest in comics entirely to manga.*

ED: Yeah, well, that was what most of them were into, yes.

GG: *So let me ask you this. You had*

artists who wanted to be cartoonists but artists who wanted to be different kinds of cartoonists. Manga, superhero, and however you would describe yourself. Could the same curriculum apply to all of you?

ED: There are some little tricky bits. You know, I'd get pretty cranky because sometimes we'd have an inking assignment to do a Batman story or whatever. But most of the

time, in all honesty, if people would just think outside their genre a little bit more, then everybody would do way better work. So if the manga kids *would* think about using some more darks, or the superhero kids would think about using some more, I don't know, doing something good... [*Laughs*] Then everyone would probably be better off. ... It wasn't too much of a hassle. Everybody was pretty tolerant of

THIS SPREAD, FROM SKETCHBOOK.

each other.

There would be basic drawing classes, and then there'd be inking classes and penciling classes, scripting, storyboarding, stuff like that.

GG: *Can you single out some of your better teachers that you learned from?*

ED: The department head John Lowe is very good. Ted Stearn taught there for a while. And he was a great teacher.

GG: *What did he teach?*

ED: Storyboarding, Intro to Sequential, Cartooning... a lot of stuff. I had some classes with Linda Medley, who taught there for a

year. I don't know if she'd want that to be mentioned in an interview, though. She was a wonderful teacher to have.

GG: *What did she teach?*

ED: I took Alternative Comics and Pencilling/Inking 1 from her, and I think she taught some intro classes. They have these basic classes you go through, and all the teachers kind of move around within them.

GG: *When you entered the school, did you know what kind of cartooning you wanted to do?*

ED: I didn't know... It was pretty silly that I went to SCAD; the decision that prompted me to go there was ridiculous. I just wanted to

make mini-comics for the rest of my life, and who the heck goes to college just to make mini-comics? It's not very sensible. But I went, and it turned out that I actually liked doing comics enough to try to do it in a more professional way. But when I showed up I was all brash and sassy and, you know, just wanting to say "Fuck the man" with my Xerox machine powers.

GG: *Well, that seems like the right attitude to enter college with.*

ED: [*Laughs*] Yeah, probably. It wasn't very nice for the people around me that first year... I did a lot of sneering and lip-curling, and...

GG: *You were intolerably brassy.*

ED: Oh, yeah.

GG: *You actually did three comics in '06. Which is reasonably prolific.*

ED: Well, some of those were left over from '05. And *Bugbear* was a joint mini with Drew.

GG: *They were published in '06, but that's right, you could have done them earlier. And they were* The Beast Mother, Mattie and Dodi, *and* Bugbear. *Which was the first one?*

ED: I think some of my short stories in *Bugbear* would have been the earliest. After that was *Beast Mother*, and some more *Bugbear* shorts, and then *Mattie and Dodi* would have been the last.

GG: *So* Mattie and Dodi *would have been after* Beast Mother.

ED: Yeah. [*Pause.*] But it's not as good. [*Laughter.*]

GG: *Well, I didn't want to say that, but...*

ED: I figured I'd say it for you, so you wouldn't have to.

GG: *I appreciate that, I wish all interview subjects were this accommodating. [Davis laughs] Before I get into that, let me ask you how your drawing evolved. I gather that it probably evolved during your period at SCAD. What did you draw like before you entered SCAD, and how did that evolve into what you're do-*ing now? *I noticed in* Bugbear *that you're a stylistic chameleon, you don't have one particular approach.*

ED: Well, uh...

GG: *I know that question is a little discursive, but...*

ED: No, I'm just trying to think. I started out learning how to draw people a little better, but I still was just using clear lines, and I was totally unable to use any blacks. This is really boring. So then I started to try to use more spot blacks and I worked on that for a while. I had a basic grasp of anatomy and a basic grasp of light and shadow, and since then I've just been trying to figure out what the heck I want to draw like. It's tricky because, each story... To me, I don't understand people who can draw in the same style over and over. I'd like to be able to do that. But any story I want to do seems to require an utterly different set of images. For any given story, I have sheaves and sheaves of sketches just trying to figure out what I want the style to be like.

GG: *So you tailor the drawing to each particular story.*

ED: Yeah, I can't help it... I never seem to be able to draw any two stories in the same way.

GG: *That's interesting. What artists were you looking at throughout your period at SCAD? Because it seems to me that you were not only influenced by cartoonists, but possibly by illustrators as well.*

ED: Hmm... I'm trying to think. I'm into just about anybody who's good. When I started dating Drew,

I got into doing much more chunky line work, because that was what he was doing at the time. Then we met this guy named Chris Wright, who, if you haven't seen any of his stuff, he's just… Oh, he did a story in *Blood Orange*. And he's just an incredible artist. He's phenomenal. As soon as we started hanging out with Chris, both me and Drew suddenly wanted to do crosshatching, because that's what Chris Wright does.

GG: *So what other cartoonists influenced you during your formative years at SCAD? I assume you read a lot of comics.*

ED: Yeah, well, you know, all of them. God, that's so irritating to say. Dan Clowes. Lyonel Feininger. Osamu Tezuka. Lewis Trondheim. Lat. Thomas Herpich. Rutu Modan. David B. Dan Zettwoch and Vanessa Davis, · recently. Tove Jansson is a huge influence, but that's been since I was really little…

GG: *The interesting thing is that I don't think that one could look at your work and really pick out any concrete stylistic influences…*

ED: I hope so. I get pretty self-conscious about that sometimes.

GG: *However you've been influenced by artists, you've clearly assimilated that, and turned whatever their influence is into your own voice.*

ED: Well, thank you. I worry about that frequently, actually, because I feel like it stands out; I say, "This is my Chris-Wright-wannabe phase" or, "This is my Gilbert-Hernandez-wannabe phase." [*Groth laughs.*] Which, of course, is ongoing. I'll never, never get out of my Gilbert-Hernandez-wannabe phase.

GG: *Is that right? What is it about Gilbert's work you like?*

ED: It's just beautiful. I love the chunky, fresh line work, and the figures are always so… so bouncy. I get into fights, actually, because everybody's so into Jaime! And I really like Jaime's art, don't get me wrong. But I'm just a Gilbert girl, I guess. People would say, "Oh, Jaime, he's the man." And I'd say, "You don't know what you're talking about! Look at this line work! Look at this texture he's put on the sky! That's fantastic!"

GG: *That's pretty great.*

Of the three books you put out in '06, I was most blown away by The Beast Mother. *Can you tell me how you conceptualized that and what was the thinking that went into that?*

ED: Well, for me, with short stories at least, it's like in one moment they don't exist, and then the next moment they do.

GG: *It sort of pops fully formed into your head?*

ED: A little bit. There's a lot of tweaking around. I was in this really rotten psychology class, so I did a lot of doodling. I did a drawing of a beast, the Beast Mother, covered with little babies. And once you do a picture like that, it's almost like there's only one story to be told, you know? It seems perfectly obvious. I came home and said, "Drew, Drew, I have this great idea for a story." I explained it to him and he said, "Well, I don't get it." [*Laughter.*] And I said, "Oh, just wait, and I promise you it'll make sense when I draw it." And I drew it. And it made some sort of sense, I guess.

GG: *What I found interesting were two things. One is how, as the story unfolds, it eventually upends your expectations. Initially it looks like the Beast Mother is protecting this brood and that this guy is hunting down their maternal guardian, and you don't really know why, so I think your sympathy lies with her. And then, you pull the ol' switcheroo, and it turns out that somehow she acquired all of these children, illegitimately, one assumes, and this guy was doing something of a good deed by reconciling them with their mothers. And then, at the end, you still feel somewhat ambivalent. I don't want to put thoughts into your head or words into your mouth, but, were you trying for that sort of ambiguity?*

ED: Yeah. One of the things I try to do most is to convey a sense of moral ambiguity in my comics. There's obviously pure good and pure bad in the world, but I've never experienced any of it. My own life experiences have been more convoluted. There just aren't good guys and bad guys. Most of the time it's just people trying to do their best, and it doesn't always work out. So the kinds of stories that interest me are

ones that don't really have a moral, but where the main characters are just having these experiences and doing the best that they can.

I did want to have the viewer kind of flip-flop in their own opinion of the situation just so they could kind of... I was hoping you'd walk away not really feeling comfortable judging it one way or another, not having harsh feelings for either the hunter or the Beast Mother.

GG: *Now, is this a perspective that you've taken from the fiction you read, or does it come purely from your observation of life, this sense of complexity and the need to express*

it? Is that the kind of work you read, or that you value?

ED: It's the kind of thing that seems the most interesting to me. As for fiction that I read... I used to read a lot more. But then I became kind of a workaholic. And it's hard to get in as much reading as I might want. But I mean, with literature, it's hardly ever cut-and-dry. I think comics still are stuck in this sort of... They're still kind of childlike, often times. So people have more expectations of there being a good guy and a bad guy, perhaps, than with proper literature.

GG: Mattie and Dodi *is a more con-*

temporary story about a relationship, and again what I liked about this was just how fraught it was with conflicting emotions and ambiguity. Can you tell me how you came upon doing this, and what your intent was?

ED: Well, my grandmother had Parkinson's, so she was in a similar situation as the grandfather in the story. She wasn't able to move or talk for many, many years... that was the personal experience aspect. And I've felt like both Dodi and Mattie at times. So I just cobbled all that together into this odd story. I still like a lot of bits of it okay, but it was problematically ambitious, I think. I guess I'm too young to do stories like that.

GG: *Because you lack the experience?*

ED: I don't know... I feel like it's a problem a lot of young alternative cartoonists have. When they write about high school or part-time jobs, stuff that's in their personal experience, is all really honest and good. But when they try to write about "adult situations" it feels like they're faking it, in a weird way. I mean, they're trying their best, it's not like they're trying to fool anyone. I definitely just felt like I was kind of getting out of my league with *Mattie and Dodi.* It's the classic cartoonist tragedy.

GG: *I thought, to tell you the truth, that your take was remarkably mature. I'm not sure how old you are.*

ED: Twenty-four.

GG: *Twenty-four. I think it's really remarkable for someone your age to have exhibited this degree of empathy.*

ED: Well, thanks. I still think it's an okay story, I just...

GG: *You can really feel Mattie's ambivalence toward the guy, whose name I forget.*

ED: I forget it, too. Sometimes I think it's Mike. But I think it's Dave, actually.

GG: *You're the author, so it can be*

whatever you want it to be.

ED: ... Call him Roy.

GG: *There's an ambivalence that she's clearly feeling toward him, as if she's going through the motions, and she's far more devoted to Dodi and her grandfather and their home than she is to him. And you can also feel his pain, because he clearly wants...*

ED: He's really being put through the wringer. He's trying his best, the poor bastard.

GG: *Exactly. And all that comes across, that complex triangle. And you did it in whatever it was, 24 pages or so, without feeling forced or strained or artificial. There was a real naturalism to it.*

ED: Well, thank you. It was all right. I think it suffered because I actually came up with the idea for it when I was 19. I had a lot of sketches, the story outlined, and then I just sat on it. I finally finished it years later for my senior project. It was like taking this enormous dump that you'd had sitting inside you for your entire college career. Finally

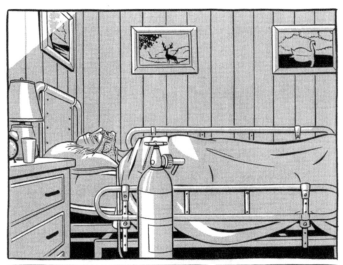

GG: *Well, if I may say so, it's more than luck... It must be hard to consciously be aware of that, because I think a lot of this must come from some deep well within you that you're not even aware of yourself...*

ED: Hmm...

GG: *Or not?*

ED: I guess you have, again, this kernel of a nugget of an idea. You say, "Okay, this guy is helping these wicked monsters. What's that about? What's this story about?" Then the story unfolds, and your main task is to try, to the best of your ability, to turn it into something other people will understand. And a lot of the time it's not successful. I showed the "Seven Sacks" story to a lot of folks, and everybody came away with different ideas of what it was about. I don't know if that's good or bad. The control freak in me is pretty bothered by how little control I have over other people's interpretations of the story. But if it wasn't complicated, it wouldn't be interesting.

GG: *I would say people's conflicting reactions to your stories is a testament to the complexity you were able to evoke. It seems to me that "Seven Sacks" springs from a single idea, and the success or failure of it hinges on the telling of it.*

ED: That was scary. That was a terrifying story to write.

GG: *And why is that? Because you*

you think, "If I don't do it now, it's just going to stay in there and calcify." [*Laughs*] Your senior project is supposed to be this big thing, so I thought, "Well, I can just shit this sucker out and see how it goes."

GG: *Did any particular class or teacher encourage that strip?*

ED: No, not really. I got a lot of nice feedback about it, but... I mean, I went into senior project already saying, "This is what I want to do." I got a lot of help from Drew, of course. We do everything together, pretty much. I really ought to just

credit him on all my comics as being a co-author, because we work together so much. Also my friend Nate Neal, who does *The Sanctuary*, was a super-big help with it.

GG: *And now, in your two MOME stories, again, the thing I love so much about the work is how fraught with mystery they are; when you finish reading them, you're not entirely sure what they meant, but you know they meant something.*

ED: If I'm lucky they mean something... I'm kind of keeping my fingers crossed.

were afraid you wouldn't be able to convey what you wanted?

ED: Some things you just have let the reader decide on their own, and you don't have too much control. But, in that story it's vital that the reader is at least curious about what's in the sacks, and scared about it too. If you draw too much attention to it, then it's too obvious, and if you don't draw enough attention to it, they miss it completely. People read comics really fast, you know? A lot of information is lost. A lot of times I'll read a comic, and then I read it again a couple years later and say, "Oh, I didn't even notice that entire aspect." You have got to make it, as much as you can, so the reader picks up on what needs to be picked up on right away. That was tricky. I wanted people to be scared of what was in the sacks but not 100% certain.

GG: *Right, what was going on with them.*

ED: Yeah.

GG: *That's gotta be the high wire act, which is, you don't want to just walk the reader through the story, so that everything is clearly articulated and you're simply manipulating the reader through a scenario. But it's got to be clear enough so that the reader doesn't lose track of what's going on. Okay, so tell me what you thought "Seven Sacks" was about?*

ED: Well, when you say it out loud it sounds so cheesy, you know? In real life, I talk a lot, I'm a yapper...

GG: *Oh yeah?*

ED: Oh yeah. In case you haven't noticed on this interview.

GG: *I should have just had Drew hide a tape recorder at dinner sometime.*

ED: No, it would be totally uninteresting, I guarantee. [*Laughs.*] Nobody wants to hear whatever it is I'm talking about, including me. It's totally boring to listen to. So, often with my comics I'm trying to figure out the core of whatever ideas I'm having at that point in my life, which I'm not able to articulate through words. So putting them back into words again is probably going to be less successful than one would hope.

GG: *That's why you did the comic in the first place, to do more than merely express an idea, so I know what I'm asking in a way defeats the point...*

ED: I guess it was like a cheesy, like... It was trying to talk about how... Well, not everybody would agree with this, of course, but... And I think partially it's just 'cause I'm in the process of growing up, and opening my eyes more to what's going on around me, but... the world's in a pretty nasty state, you know—

GG: *Indeed.*

ED: ...things are not going so great for the Earth... and for Mankind. And living in America, in this super-well-to-do, protected nation, it's really easy to ignore all that. Even if you know what's going on, it's easier to turn away and pretend it's not happening. I know that's the same sort of sentiment you see in cheesy TV ads all the time. But I was trying to illustrate it in a more roundabout way. In the end — it wasn't a very long story, it's kind of hard to do in only 12 pages — but, you're supposed to empathize with the ferryman and understand why he chose to pretend nothing bad was going on.

GG: *Yeah, yeah, the question seems to be: What is his responsibility?*

ED: Yeah, what is his responsibility? He couldn't do anything. He's helpless. And what's our responsibility? [*Groth laughs*] To put it totally obviously and cheesily.

GG: *You articulated that question in a very undogmatic way.*

ED: Well, it's not like I have... If I was off giving mouth-to-mouth to lepers, maybe I could tell other people what they should be doing with their lives. But I'm just a cartoonist.

GG: *You don't have the answers.*

ED: No, I don't. I'm not doing anything, myself, so...

GG: *Well, having strips published in MOME is almost like giving mouth-to-mouth to lepers. [Davis laughs] Now, in "Stick and String," which is in this issue, this was similarly ambiguous, and I wasn't entirely sure what to make of it [Davis laughs], except that two people connected, finally.*

ED: Yeah.

GG: *The problem always with inter-*

preting art is that you're imposing a sort of literal-mindedness on something that ought to exist as itself, so I'm guilty of that. But on the other hand I think that's a natural response to art, trying to make sense of it. But two people connected to each other, and the girl seems to have missed her clan or friends or whatever, and then was brought back to the man she met, through the beauty of his music. Is that something close to what you were going for?

ED: My intention was that the girl in story had almost been hypnotized by the guitarist's music. Neither of them realized what was going on. He just thought she was falling in love with him. He thought she would... She kind of becomes a human, her antlers go away. So he thinks she's human now, and they're in love, and that's the way it's gonna be. But it was a mistake, you know? He had accidentally tricked her. Not even purposefully.

GG: *Beguiled her.*

ED: Yeah. And then, in the end, he's fearful because without the beguil-

ing music, she's still what she always was.

GG: *She is who she is.*

ED: Yeah, and she's dangerous. I don't know. I'm still not sure what I think of it because I finished it pretty recently. So... I don't know, I guess it's sort of about *relationships...*

GG: *That old saw.*

ED: Yeah, pretty much. I tried to tell the first part like a fable, so you think it's going to be just a simple story with a happy ending. Again, using the old fable schtick. But in the end it's more complicated... Just like relationships! [*Laughter.*]

GG: *Tell me about it. Now, in both your* MOME *strips, can you tell me the medium you used? Was that watercolor?*

ED: It was actually concentrated watercolor dyes. They're really water soluble, and they bleed a lot. In "Seven Sacks" I did the linework in dye and then did washes over the top, so everything bled and ran together. In "Stick and String" I did normal inks, with an overlay of the watercolor dyes. They're real easy and they blend pretty good.

GG: *And the color scheme is the same in both, a kind of burnt orange.*

ED: Yeah, pretty similar. The nice thing about the dyes is that they separate out into a bunch of differ-

ent colors, so you can get a lot of varieties from just one tone.

GG: *To finish it off let me ask you: What cartoonists are you looking at now for inspiration and enjoyment?*

ED: Well, "I'm glad you asked, Gary." I have recently decided — I often recently decide things — But I currently think that Joann Sfar is just about the best cartoonist in the world.

GG: *Ah!* The Rabbi's Cat, *and...*

ED: I particularly like *Klezmer* and *Vampire Loves*. I haven't even seen most of his stuff because it hasn't been translated yet. He's just extraordinary. He draws and writes so ecstatically. Everybody should read his stuff. It upsets Drew. [*Laughs.*] Drew often says "If Joann Sfar and I were both hanging from a cliff, [*laughter*] who would you save?'

GG: *[Laughter.] I can understand where that would be worrisome.*

M

SO? THINK YOU PICKED THE RIGHT ONE?

YEAH. IT'S REALLY GOOD. THANKS.

HEY, NO PROBLEM... I **LIKE** SCOOPING ICE CREAM. I MEAN, IT'S HARD TO HATE **THAT** PART, RIGHT?

IT'S WASHING ALL THESE DISHES THAT SUCKS. THERE'S ALWAYS A PILE OF THEM... I'M SO ANAL ABOUT CLEANING THEM THAT THEY TAKE FOREVER... BUT THE **REAL** PROBLEM'S WHEN I **FINISH** THEM.

...BECAUSE THEN I'M SO HAPPY WITH MYSELF THAT I LET MYSELF TAKE A BREAK FROM THEM. AND IN NO TIME: TA DA! I'M BACK IN THE SAME BOAT.

THAT REMINDS ME OF... DID YOU SEE THAT "MR. DANGEROUS" WHERE FARMER GREG LOSES HIS AMNESIA, WITH THE MANURE...

NO, I'VE HONESTLY NEVER SEEN THAT SHOW, WHICH SUCKS BECAUSE PEOPLE ARE ALWAYS QUOTING IT...

I END UP KNOWING A BUNCH OF LINES TO A SHOW I'VE NEVER SEEN.

WELL, YOU KNOW THE BASIC CHARACTERS THEN, RIGHT? MR. DANGEROUS AND FARMER GREG AND...

NO, I MEAN, MR. DANGEROUS, SURE, BUT WHAT IS HE? HE'S SOME KIND OF TIKI DUDE OR SOMETHING?

NO, HE'S JUST...WEIRD. I GUESS WHAT HE IS IS SORT OF THE PLOT OF THE SHOW... HE'S GOT THIS NEIGHBOR, FARMER GREG...

THE SHOW NEVER SAYS THEY'RE ANYTHING MORE THAN NEIGHBORS, BUT SOMETIMES I THINK FARMER GREG IS MR. DANGEROUS' DAD... BUT ANYWAY, FARMER GREG STAYS OUT IN THE SUN TOO LONG ONE DAY AND GETS AMNESIA. AND IN THE AMNESIA, HE FORGETS WHO MR. DANGEROUS IS...

HE THINKS HE'S A WEED, A RABBIT, SOMETHING HE HAS TO TAKE CARE OF, A BABY, WHATEVER... IT'S DIFFERENT EVERY EPISODE.

AMNESIA FROM STANDING IN THE SUN?

WHATEVER. IT'S A GOOD SHOW.

BUT WHAT YOU WERE SAYING, WITH THE DISHES, JUST REMINDED ME OF THIS EPISODE WHERE FARMER GREG GETS A WHIFF OF THIS WEIRD MANURE.

AND JUST FOR A SECOND THE AMNESIA'S GONE, AND HE REALIZES, "HEY, THIS IS MY NEIGHBOR," AND THEY'RE OKAY WITH EACH OTHER. FOR A SECOND, EVERYTHING'S GREAT.

BUT THEN MR. DANGEROUS IS SO HAPPY AT BEING RECOGNIZED THAT HE JUMPS AND HE KNOCKS A VASE ON TO FARMER GREG'S HEAD... AND **DUH**, THE AMNESIA COMES RIGHT BACK.

HUH. WEIRD. PROBABLY NOT REALLY MY SPEED. BUT IT SOUNDS INTERESTING.

YEAH...

YEAH, I GUESS IT'S PRETTY INTERESTING.

SO...
UM...

HEY, SO...
I'M CLOSING
UP NOW,
BUT,,

OH. I'M
SORRY.

NO, I WAS GOING TO
SAY... DO YOU WANT
TO HANG OUT? IF
YOU'RE NOT DOING
ANYTHING.

OH...
WELL..

WE COULD WATCH
A MOVIE AT
MY PLACE OR
SOMETHING,

SURE...
OKAY.

COOL. JUST
CHILL OUT FOR
A COUPLE MINUTES
WHILE I CLOSE
THINGS UP.

SO, IT'S JUST BRIDGEPORT, AND THEN A COUPLE MILES, YOU'RE OKAY TO FOLLOW ME?

SURE.

OKAY... OKAY.

LIGHTEN UP! HE'S REALLY **NICE**. IT'S NOT LIKE HE SAID SOMETHING SHITTY LIKE, "THAT SHOW SOUNDS FUCKIN' **DUMB**." HE'S NOT ERIC AT LEAST...

WHY DO YOU EXPECT PEOPLE TO REWRITE THE UNIVERSE IN THE FIRST FIVE SENTENCES?

THERE'S TONS OF STUFF **I** HAVEN'T SEEN. MICHAEL'S **ALWAYS** MENTIONING MOVIES THAT I HAVEN'T... MICHAEL. JESUS. WHAT THE FUCK AM I DOING?

WELL, HE'S IN SAN FRANCISCO ANYWAY, PORTLAND. WHATEVER...

JESUS, WHY DID I LEAVE HIM THAT MESSAGE?

GREAT. NOW I NEED TO FART... PERFECT.

Please, TALK TO THE HAND.

SO HERE'S THE DEAL-O. I drew a little face on the back of my, um, hand, and I thought _whoa_, I just _love_ how that turned out, it's so _cute_! Then I had an idea: if I block _your_ head with it, it's as though I'm just talking to this _adorable_ little dude on the back of my hand, whose face isn't, like, _ass ugly_. I mean, it _totally_ solves the problem of me hating _talking_ to you because of your face. Talk about _fun_, right?